Katharine the Almost Great

The Artsy-Fartsy Auction

by Lisa Mullarkey
illustrated by Phyllis Harris

visit us at www.abdopublishing.com

To the students and staff at EJ Patten School in Perth Amboy, NJ, who inspired this story: You rock! —LM
To Paige, my great art buddy! —PH

Published by Magic Wagon, a division of the ABDO Group, PO Box 398166, Minneapolis, Minnesota 55439.

Printed in the United States of America, North Mankato, Minnesota.
092011
012012

This book contains at least 10% recycled materials.

Text by Lisa Mullarkey
Illustrations by Phyllis Harris
Edited by Stephanie Hedlund and Rochelle Baltzer
Interior layout and design by Jaime Martens
Cover design by Jaime Martens

Library of Congress Cataloging-in-Publication Data
Mullarkey, Lisa.
The artsy-fartsy auction / by Lisa Mullarkey ; illustrated by Phyllis Harris.
p. cm. -- (Katharine the Almost Great)
Summary: The school is having a secret silent auction of student art works to raise money for charity and Katharine is annoyed because someone keeps bidding against her and also worried that her cousin Crockett will not get the item he really wants.
ISBN 978-1-61641-829-8
1. Art auctions--Juvenile fiction. 2. Money-making projects for children--Juvenile fiction. 3. Schools--Juvenile fiction. 4. Cousins--Juvenile fiction. 5. Friendship--Juvenile fiction. [1. Auctions--Fiction. 2. Art--Fiction. 3. Fund raising--Fiction. 4. Schools--Fiction. 5. Cousins--Fiction. 6. Friendship--Fiction.] I. Harris, Phyllis, 1962- ill. II. Title. III. Series: Mullarkey, Lisa. Katharine the Almost Great.
PZ7.M91148Ar 2012
813.6--dc23 2011026386

CONTENTS

CHAPTER 1

Seeing Red

"Roy G. Biv would be proud," said Mrs. Dee to Crockett. "Your painting is bright and cheery."

Crockett dipped his brush in his paint. He swooshed it over his green pear. His fruit bowl was bright and cheery.

Mine was not cheery. It was dreary. Dreary with a capital *D*.

Crockett leaned over. "What's with all the red?" he asked.

I shrugged and stared at my painting. I had red apples, red grapes, red peaches, and red raspberries.

"Who's Roy G. Biv?" I asked.

Vanessa sighed. "Don't you remember anything? We learned that in kindergarten."

I tap, tap, tapped my paintbrush on the table. Kindergarten was a long time ago. "Was it a composer?" I asked.

Vanessa laughed.

Crockett laughed.

I scrunched my face. "Was it a scientist?"

Then Matthew laughed. A lot.

It was not a chuckle moment. I tossed my paintbrush on the table. "Is anyone going to tell me?"

Mrs. Dee drew a picture on the board. "It's a way to remember the colors of the rainbow." She pointed to each color. "Red, Orange, Yellow, Green, Blue, Indigo, and Violet. Roy G. Biv."

My cheeks matched my red, red fruit. "Did you know that kiwifruit came from China? They were called Chinese gooseberries. Farmers in New Zealand changed the name to kiwi after their country's bird."

My calendar of 365 useless facts never let me down!

Vanessa waved to her kiwi. "Hello, Chinese gooseberry!" Then she pointed her nose in the air. "Even people in China and New Zealand know about Roy G. Biv."

This is what I wanted to say:

"Mind your own business, Miss Priss-A-Poo. Your kiwi looks like a watermelon."

But Mrs. Dee was at the next table. So, this is what I really said:

"Oh."

Mrs. Dee studied Vanessa's painting. She held it in the air to show the class.

"Look at Vanessa's pears. What lovely shades of green." She pointed to the kiwi. "I love your watermelon!"

Now it was my turn to laugh. Vanessa gave me her grumpy eyes.

Mrs. Dee cleared her throat. "I have a special announcement. We're having an art auction."

Crockett's eyes lit up. "We had an auction in Junior Rangers last year. I bid the most on a compass, so I won it."

Mrs. Dee wiped a blob of paint off of her nose. Poor Mrs. Dee! She always looked like a rainbow threw up all over her clothes.

"We will be having a silent auction," she said. "You'll be given numbers—secret numbers. Only you, your parents, and Mrs. Ammer will know what your number is. If you see a piece of artwork you want, write your number on the card. Not your name. Then, write down what you're willing to pay for it."

She pointed to Vanessa's painting. "Let's say Matthew wanted to buy this for one dollar. He'd write his number and $1.00 on the card. Someone may come along and write $2.00 on the next line with his number. If anyone else wanted it, the bid would need to be more than two dollars. At the end of the week, the highest bidder wins."

"Here's a sample from a first grader." She held up a collage with pieces of tissue paper mashed together. "Isn't it pretty?"

I wasn't impressed. Not one itty-bitty bit.

And I wasn't the only one. "Who'd pay for that?" asked Miss Priss-A-Poo. "Even Ka—" She smooshed her lips together. Then she finished by saying, “Even I could make it.”

Mrs. Dee read the name on the back. “Someone who wants to own a Dylan Thomas original will pay for it.”

“Dylan was my reading buddy!” I shouted. “Maybe I’ll bid on it!”

“I hope you do, Katharine,” said Mrs. Dee. “All money will be donated to charity.” She wiped her painty hands on her painty pants. “This month, five students from each class will donate something to the auction.”

Vanessa sat up extra tall. “I’ll donate my painting.” Then she frowned. “I’ll have to fix my kiwi first.”

Mrs. Dee patted Vanessa on the shoulder. “I’ve already picked five names out of a hat.” As she rattled off the names, I crossed my fingers.

“Diego, Drew . . .”

Two down. Three to go. Since my fingers weren't bringing me luck, I crossed my legs, too.

"Tamara, Rebecca, and . . ."

I sucked in my breath and crossed my arms and eyes.

"Katharine."

"I won! I won!" I shouted.

Mrs. Dee laughed. "Everyone's a winner. All students will have a turn to donate to the auction this year."

Vanessa huff-a-puffed. "I didn't want to be in this artsy-fartsy auction anyway."

Ha! She couldn't fool me.

I added more grapes to my bowl. Now I had green grapes, red grapes, and purplicious grapes.

But Vanessa had grapes I didn't have . . . sour grapes!

CHAPTER 2

Attitude vs. Sassitude

"You're donating that?" asked Crockett at the dinner table.

I held up my masterpiece. "It's a per-fect-o papier-mâché popcorn bowl."

Crockett raised one eyebrow. "It would be if Jack hadn't chewed a hole right there."

"That makes it scary. Perfect for scary movie nights," I said. "Who wouldn't want the bite marks of Jackula himself?"

Crockett raised his other eyebrow. "It says *Made by Katarine*."

Mom laughed. "You spelled your name wrong. It looks funny."

"Then it's perfect to use if you're watching a comedy, too." I flashed Crockett a super-duper smile. "It really is a fab-u-lo-so bowl."

Mom agreed. "I love how you painted a bottle of Monsters-Be-Gone Spray on the bottom."

Jack grabbed the bowl and banged it on my head.

"Ouch!" I tugged the bowl away from him. "I need Brother-Be-Gone spray."

Jack kicked and screamed.

Dad tried not to smile. "Katharine, apologize to the little guy."

I put my hand on my forehead and used my best Penelope Parks voice. "Did Jack ever apologize for hitting me? Nooooo! Did he ever apologize for puking green stuff on me? Nooooo! Did he ever say he was sorry for biting my toes? I think not!" I pretended to cry.

Jack laughed at my A+ performance.

"Aw, Penelope!" said Aunt Chrissy. "You know Jack thinks your little piggies are tasty!"

I giggled. Penelope Parks is my most very favorite actress! "I think I'll raise at least fifty dollars for the auction." I took my Luscious Lemon Lip Gloss out of my pocket and slathered it on my lips. "Maybe even a hundred smack-a-roos!"

My parents call me Katharine the *Almost* Great. They say I'm a work-in-progress. Maybe if someone bids mucho mega moola on my bowl, they'll call me Katharine the Great.

"Good luck," said Mom.

"Good luck," said Dad.

Crockett patted me on the back. "You're going to need it."

Crockett was just kidding . . . I think!

When I brought my bowl into school the next day, everyone gathered around my desk.

"Here it is," I announced. "My donation."

Miss Priss-A-Poo picked it up. "You're donating this?"

I gave her my you-better-not-say-anything-mean-to-me look.

"I love it," said Vanessa. "I'm going to bid on it. I love to watch movies and munch on popcorn." Then she added, "As long as they're not movies about Jackula or Frankiestein."

I pointed to the Monsters-Be-Gone picture. "That's why I painted this on it. Just in case."

Mrs. Bingsley rushed over to me. "Bring your donation to Mrs. Dee in the cafeteria. She's waiting for it."

I zip-a-zoomed straight there and took a sneak peek at all of the art projects. There were all sorts of masks, painted ceramic tiles, clay pots, and sculptures made out of junk.

"There's lots more coming," said Mrs. Dee. "I think we're going to raise lots of money this month." She glanced at the clock. "You better get back to class. The teachers are handing out bid numbers right after they take attendance. You want to be sure to get one."

I skedaddled out of there and skipped back to class. Mrs. Bingsley was waiting with my envelope in her hand. It said *Katharine* on the outside and a slip of paper with *#100* was on the inside.

"You can preview the art at lunch today, kids. Bidding starts tomorrow," Mrs. Bingsley announced.

Everyone cheered.

"Remember," said Mrs. Bingsley, "Mrs. Ammer doesn't want anyone sharing numbers. No one is allowed to discuss bids. We don't want any hurt feelings. Understand?"

We nodded. Mrs. Ammer was our principal. Everyone called her Ammer the Hammer. If you didn't follow her rules, she'd nail you.

After lunch, Rebecca, Tamara, Vanessa, and I walked around the tables. There was so much to see.

"Here's Dylan's picture," said Rebecca. "It's kind of cute for a first grader."

"Jack will love it," I said. "It matches his room."

"It would look great in Frankie's room, too," said Vanessa. "Maybe I'll bid on it." She smirked.

That smirk was for me! I crossed my arms. "He was *my* Author's Tea buddy."

But Vanessa wasn't listening. She had rushed over to another table that was surrounded by girls who were trying to see something.

Rebecca, Tamara, and I wanted to see what was going on. We finally pushed our way to the front. That's when we saw it.

A portrait of Penelope Parks!

It was propped up on a gold easel. At the top of the painting, it said "Penelope Parks has an A+ Attitude." That was the title of her last movie.

Penelope looked shimmery.

Shiny.

Glitzy.

Glimmery.

"It's per-fect-o," I sighed. "I'm going to bid on it."

Rebecca nodded. "I'm bidding on it, too."

"Count me in," said Tamara.

Vanessa took a deep breath. "It's beautiful." Then she put her hands on her hips and tossed her hair all around. "I'm not only going to bid on it, I'm going to win it." Then she sashayed away.

Just. Like. That.

I looked back at the painting.

Penelope did have an A+ attitude.

Vanessa did not.

Nope. Miss Priss-A-Poo had a bad case of sassitude.

Penelope Parks
has an
A+
attitude.

CHAPTER 3

The Bidding Begins

Before school started the next day, I cornered Crockett on the playground. I asked, "How much money do you have?"

He pulled his pockets inside out. "None here. But twenty-four dollars at home."

I sat on a swing. "I have seventeen dollars. If we put our money together," I quickly did the math. "We'll have forty-three dollars for the auction."

"First of all," said Crockett, "we'd only have forty-one dollars. Second of all, last time I gave you money to buy us something, you came home with socks."

"What's wrong with socks? You wear socks, don't you?" I asked.

"Not ones with glitter, sparkles, and hearts," Crockett replied.

"But this is different!" I said. "I really, really, really want the P—"

Crockett covered his ears. "Katharine! We're not allowed to talk about it." He dashed over to the basketball court.

Sometimes it's hard to have a cousin who never breaks the rules. Crockett is a fair and square kind of kid.

When we walked inside, I ducked into the cafeteria and poked around the tables.

Mom was poking around them, too. "Sweetie Pie!" She held out her latest creation: an oatmeal and banana breakfast cookie. “There are so many fantastic art pieces here. I wish I could bid on them.”

I popped the cookie into my mouth. “Why can’t you?”

“I suppose I could. But I feel the same way I felt when Crockett and Vanessa both ran for president. I wore each of their campaign buttons, remember? As a school employee, I’d feel terrible bidding on one kid’s artwork and not another.”

“You’re a fair and square kind of mom.” I pointed to her cookies. “And you’re one smart cookie.”

Then I grabbed her hand and led her to the fifth grade tables. “Vanessa is driving me bonkers. She is not a fair and square kind of girl. Yesterday, she said she wanted to bid on my bowl. But then she said she might bid on Dylan’s collage. You know why? Because she knew I wanted to bid on it. Now she wants to bid on this." I pointed to the Penelope Parks painting. "Just because I'm bidding on it. She's a copycat."

Mom studied the painting. "I'm sure all the girls are bidding on it." Then she sighed. "Don't you think you have enough Penelope Parks junk?"

I almost choked on her cookie. *Junk?!* "Mother, Penelope shines! She simply sparkles. You can never have enough of Penelope Parks!" I kicked my glittery sneaker into the air. "Are these junk? Look how the stars sparkle."

Mom flicked a piece of glitter off her apron.

I puckered my lips. "I'm wearing Penelope's Luscious Lemon Lip Gloss. Do my lips look like junk?" Then I remembered my Penelope Parks underwear. "In fact," I whispered, "I have on Penelope Parks undies."

I looked around to make sure we were alone. "The ones with the bumblebees that say 'Bee All That You Can Bee.' How can you call my underwear junk?"

Mom shrugged. "I suppose beauty is in the eye of the beholder."

I pulled a pencil out of my backpack. "I'm going to be the first bidder. I'm a lucky duck." I wrote down #100: $17.00. "That's all I have."

Mom erased my bid. "Start small. Bid a dollar. You can bid more later if you need to. It may not even sell for seventeen dollars."

My mom wasn't just fair and square. She was smart, too. I scribbled down #100: $1.00. Easy breezy!

Then I bit my lip. "What if Vanessa gets it?"

Mom shrugged. "Then that's the way the cookie crumbles."

After recess, I found out Vanessa wasn't going to crumble my cookie after all.

"I can't bid on your bowl, Katharine." She shoved her folder in her desk. "Or Dylan's collage or the portrait of Penelope." She opened her wallet. "I used my last ten dollars to buy a DVD last night."

"Won't your parents give you money?" I asked.

"Nope," said Vanessa. "They said I need to learn to be more responsible with my money."

This is what I wanted to say:

"Yippee! Yahoo! Nanny nanny boo hoo. See ya! Wouldn't want to be ya!"

But this is what I really said:

"You can always bid next month, Vanessa."

After that, I was so hap, hap, happy that I sharpened everyone's pencils during free time. I even let Tamara have the purplicious beanbag chair during reading. And when I heard Alex's stomach growl, I gave him my extra apple slices during snack.

But I sure got crank, crank, cranky during lunch. When I went to check out the Penelope Parks painting, there were already eight bids!

#100: $1.00

#336: $2.00

#243: $3.00

#336: $3.50

#118: $4.50

#336: $5.00

#129: $5.25

#336: $7.00

I scratched my head and looked around the room. Who was #336? Someone like me who really wanted a Penelope Parks painting, that's who! I wrote my new bid: #100: $10.00.

Take that #336, whoever you are!

But then I worried about #336 all afternoon. What if #336 had a gazillion dollars? And what if she used those gazillion dollars to buy every single Penelope Parks item on Earth? Worrying about Gazillion Dollar Girl made concentrating on math extra hard.

"Katharine? What's the answer?" Mrs. Bingsley tapped my desk. "Katharine?"

"A gazillion dollars!" I shouted.

Everyone laughed.

Everyone except Mrs. Bingsley. "So you're saying that 843 minus 761 equals a gazillion dollars?"

My face felt like my fruit bowl again. My stomach did a flip-flop belly drop. "Did you know that a ten-dollar bill only lasts about eighteen months before it gets worn out? Then the government shreds it. Like confetti."

Mrs. Bingsley sighed.

I gave another amazing fact. "But a hundred-dollar bill lasts a whole eighty-nine months!"

Mrs. Bingsley folded her arms. "Katharine, we need the answer to the problem. Do you have it?"

But I never answered her. I couldn't.

I was too busy staring at the itty-bitty paper under Vanessa's desk.

The paper said #336!

Glum Chums

Vanessa was Gazillion Dollar Girl! I suddenly felt like Godzilla. I wanted to stomp on that itty-bitty paper. I wanted to run into the cafeteria and swipe that painting off of the table and roar, "Bid on something else, Miss Priss-A-Poo!"

But I didn't. I couldn't.

Instead, I scooted my desk over a few inches and whispered in her ear. "Liar, liar, pants on fire!"

Vanessa tossed her hair from side to side. She scrunched her face. "Huh?"

"Lying makes you a Cheatie Girl."

Vanessa barked, "I am not a Cheatie Girl!"

Mrs. Bingsley looked up. "Is there a problem, girls?"

I wanted to shout: "Miss Priss-A-Poo is #336. She's Gazillion Dollar Girl." But if I did, I'd lose bidding privileges. So, I shook my head no.

Vanessa spent the rest of the afternoon trying to talk to me. When I got a drink from the water fountain, she got one, too.

"Okay," said Vanessa as she wiped water off of her chin. "You're right. I did lie."

"Aha!" I said. "I knew you were a Cheatie Girl!"

She lowered her eyes. "I lied about the breakfast oatmeal cookie. I didn't like it. It was sort of gross."

"So you lied about that, too?" I asked. "How rude! Now you're a double liar! Liar, liar pants on fire, fire."

When I got a tissue, Miss Priss-A-Poo suddenly had a sneezing fit. She rush-a-rooed over to the tissue box.

"Okay," she said again. "I lied about something else."

I folded my arms and tapped my fingers on my elbows. "I'm waiting."

"I lied about the math test last week. I didn't get 100. I got a 77."

My jaw dropped. "Now you're a triple liar. Liar, liar, liar pants on fire, fire, fire!"

Vanessa wiggled her nose and stomped away.

Before the spelling bee started, Vanessa rushed over to me. I thought she'd finally confess to being Gazillion Dollar Girl.

I thought wrong.

"Oh, yeah, Katharine. I lied another time."

I leaned in real close to get a look at her nose. I figured it would start growing any second now.

She rolled her eyes. "I lied when I said you were a good speller!" She stuck her tongue out at me.

I'd show her!

And I would have if my second spelling word wasn't *dire*.

"Dire," I repeated.

Crockett gave me two thumbs-up. He would have given me thumbs-down if he knew I hadn't studied my words last night. Or the night before.

"I know this one," whispered Vanessa to Haley.

I cracked my knuckles. "Dire," I repeated.

Vanessa whispered some more. "Dire rhymes with liar." She covered her mouth. "Oops."

"Can you spell the word, Katharine?" asked Mrs. Bingsley.

I smiled at Vanessa and nodded. "D-I-A-R."

"I'm sorry," said Mrs. Bingsley. "That's incorrect."

I glared at Vanessa. She jumped up and down. It was her turn now.

"Dire. D-I-R-E. Dire," she announced.

Everyone clapped. Except me.

Vanessa may have won the spelling bee, but I'd make sure she didn't win the painting.

After school, Crockett and I went to meet Mom in the cafeteria. Crockett walked over to one of the fifth grade tables.

I headed straight to see my Penelope painting. It was up to fifteen dollars!

#100: $1.00

#336: $2.00

#243: $3.00

#336: $3.50

#118: $4.50

#336: $5.00

#129: $5.25

#336: $7.00

#100: $10.00

#243: $11.00

#336: $13.00

#421: $13.25

#336: $15.00

I jotted down my next bid: #100: $15.50. Then I walked over to see Crockett. "What'cha looking at?"

"This." He held up a wooden box.

It looked like someone made it by gluing rectangular blocks together.

"Someone used a tool to burn the words *Junior Rangers* on the top," said Crockett. "Isn't it great?"

"Umm . . . it's a box, Crockett. We have lots of boxes at home. Big ones. Small ones. Even crushed ones, thanks to Jack."

"It's not just a box, Katharine. It's a Junior Rangers box to hold your compass."

I lifted it up to the light. "Yep. It's a box."

Crockett looked upset. "Everyone has one except me." He took a deep breath. “I need one before I go on my next camping trip.”

“Bid on this one,” I said.

He shook his head. “My dad promised he’d come visit this weekend. We’re supposed to make one then.”

That’s when I knew what was wrong. Aunt Chrissy said that Uncle Greg is great at making promises but even better at breaking them.

Crockett’s voice cracked. “I hope he comes this weekend.” Crockett put the box back on the table. Then he walked over to another group of tables. “Where’s your bowl?”

I spun around. “I guess it’s with the third grade stuff.” I grabbed his hand and dragged him across the room.

“Here it is!” he said. “Your masterpiece.”

I covered my eyes. “I can’t look. How many bids are there?”

"Just one," said Crockett.

My heart thumpity thumped. "Only one? Are you positive? Positively positive?" My stomach did a flip-flop belly drop. What if the bid was a penny? Or only fifty cents? That's not a lot of money to donate to charity. I didn't even want to see the bid. "Do you think anyone else will bid on it?"

Crockett shrugged his shoulders as he walked back over to the table with the box.

When he finally looked over, I tried to smile and wave.

But I was not in a smiley mood.

Crockett sort of waved back, but he wasn't in a smiley mood either.

We were gloomy. Glum. Glum chums.

CHAPTER 5

Bad News

"How's the auction going?" asked Dad as he scooped another meatball onto his plate at dinner. "Did you make millions off of your bowl yet?"

Jack mashed spaghetti into his hair. "No."

I gave Jack my grumpy eyes. "I didn't want to look. It's better to be surprised." I picked a strand of spaghetti off of Jack's ear.

Crockett looked at me like I had ten eyes.

But how could I tell my parents that only one person liked my artwork enough to bid on it? Then I remembered Gazillion Dollar Girl and lost my appetite. I pushed my plate away and sunk down in my chair.

"Vanessa's bidding on everything that I'm bidding on," I said.

Dad looked confused. "How do you know her number?" He twirled some pasta on his fork. "I thought the numbers were private."

"They are," said Crockett. "At least they're supposed to be." He scooped another meatball out of the pot. "Do you know it?"

"Nope." Now I was a Cheatie Girl! "But as soon as I say I like something, she says she likes it, too." I tossed Crockett a piece of bread. "I'm warning you, Crockett. You better not tell her about that box you saw. She'll bid on it."

“What box?” asked Aunt Chrissy.

“It was nothing,” said Crockett. “Just a plain box to keep junk in.”

Now I looked at Crockett like he had ten eyes.

I wiped my mouth. “If Vanessa sees you even looking at it, she’ll start bidding on it.”

“Well, she can bid on it all she wants,” said Crockett. “I’m not bidding on it.”

Dad took a sip of water. “Vanessa can bid on whatever she wants, Katharine. Everyone can. Don’t lose sight of the reason you’re having the auction. It’s to help people in need. Like I said before, it’s not a time to duke it out with Vanessa.”

“She’s not even bidding, Katharine,” said Crockett. “She doesn’t have any money.”

Ha! My mouth wanted to explode-a-rama and tell them about the Gazillion Dollar Girl drama! But I stuck my fork in my meatball and changed the subject.

"Did you know that if you wanted to cook 1 billion pounds of pasta, you'd need 2,021,452,000 gallons of water? That's enough water to fill up 75,000 Olympic-size swimming pools."

"I can't even eat all the pasta on my plate," said Mom. "I can't imagine having to cook 1 billion pounds!"

Just then, the phone rang downstairs. Aunt Chrissy jumped up. "I'm waiting for an important call. Be back in a second." She ran downstairs.

But she wasn't back in a second. Or a minute. Or even in ten minutes. She didn't come back upstairs until the dishes were done.

"Was it Dad?" asked Crockett.

Aunt Chrissy nodded. “He had an emergency come up this weekend. He can’t come.”

Crockett got up and walked to the sink. “I had plans with Johnny anyway. His dad asked if I could go on a hike with them. We’re trying to earn another Junior Rangers Wilderness Badge.” He picked up a small bucket of scraps. “Can I bring these out to Hotel Wormella?”

Hotel Wormella was Crockett’s worm compost project.

Aunt Chrissy hugged Crockett. “Sure. I’ll come with you.” I saw her give my mom a look. A do-not-ask-any-questions look.

“I’m okay, Mom. I just want to dump these in and then start my homework,” Crockett said.

Aunt Chrissy didn’t look like she believed him.

When Crockett didn't come in after ten minutes, I went out to find him. He wasn't near the compost area. He wasn't in our tree house either.

I cupped my hands and yelled, "Come out, come out, wherever you are!"

Nobody answered. But then I heard a sniff. Then a snuff. Crockett was behind the garage sitting under a tree. His eyes were watery.

"Sorry about your dad, Crockett," I whispered.

"It's okay. I sort of expected him to call and cancel," he said.

I put my arm around him.

"You're so lucky that your dad is always here, Katharine."

I nodded. "My dad is sort of like your dad," I said. "He loves you as much as he loves me and Jack."

"Yeah, I know," said Crockett. "But it's not the same."

He rested his head on the tree trunk. "Your dad planted these trees for you. With you. Your dad cheers you on when you swim. He tucks you in every night. He helps you with your math homework."

"You get to take cool vacations with your dad," I said. "And he buys you lots of cool stuff."

Crockett threw a stone across the bushes. "I don't think you get it."

But I did.

Crockett needed cheering up. And I knew the perfect person to do it.

Me!

A Plan for Crockett

The next morning, I worked on my Cheer Up Crockett Day plan before he got up for school. I grabbed the Toaster Puffs from the cabinet and plopped them on the table. Then I cut five strips of paper and wrote a joke on each one. Crockett loves jokes.

What do you call a lizard that sings? *A RAP-tile.*

Where do frogs keep their money? *In a river bank!*

What do toads drink? *Croaka-cola!*

How can you tell if a snake is a baby? *It has a rattle!*

Why does Mrs. Bingsley wear sunglasses? *Because our class is so bright!*

I wanted to sneak downstairs and put them on his nightstand. But his basement is full of critters. I do not like critters—even caged ones. So I crumpled up each joke and tossed them down the stairs.

Then I wrote him a note on a napkin. *Dear Crockett, You are the* best *cousin ever. You're my most* favorite *one, too.*

The clock said six thirty. I had a lot to do in the next thirty minutes.

By seven o'clock, I was ready. A few minutes later, I heard the squeaky steps.

"What's with all this trash?" asked Crockett.

Then I heard him laugh. And then he laughed again. He laughed each time he opened up a joke.

He ran up the steps. "Funny jokes, Katharine. Thanks!"

I poured a bowl of cereal for Crockett. "This is the last bowl of Toaster Puffs. But you can have them."

Crockett pushed the bowl toward me. "But it's your favorite cereal."

I pushed it back to him. "But I always get the last bowl. I'm trying to be more of a fair and square kind of girl."

Crockett ate those Toaster Puffs quicky quick. When he grabbed a napkin, he saw the note. "Thanks, Katharine. But you do know that I'm your only cousin, don't you?"

After breakfast, Crockett opened the cabinet under the sink. "Hey! Where's all the recycling? I have to get it out before the truck comes."

"I took it out earlier," I said. "It's not fair that you always take it out."

"Want to have a race?" I asked on our way to school. "Ready, set, go!"

Crockett's eyes lit up. I always tell him that racing makes me too sweaty. But not today! He ran so fast, he beat me to school. He even jogged backward the last few feet.

"I won!" he shouted.

I gave him two thumbs-up. "You're always a winner to me."

He sort of rolled his eyes. "Are you feeling okay? You're acting a little goofy."

I made a funny face. "Because I'm a goofball."

He laughed again. My plan was working!

During snack time, I raised my hand. "Mrs. Bingsley, may I please run an important errand?"

"An errand?" she asked. "Where do you need to go? The library?"

I shook my head. I walked over and whispered in her ear, "It's a top secret mission."

Mrs. Bingsley chewed on her lip. She sometimes does that when she's thinking. "What's the top secret mission?"

"If I told you, it wouldn't be top secret." Then I gave her my puppy dog eyes. "But it is important. It's something that would make me an extra caring student."

She kept on chewing. "Will this top secret mission take a long time to complete?"

I didn't want to be a Cheatie Girl so I said, "I don't think so. But it could take me ten minutes. Maybe twenty. But I promise, it's a good thing. A super-duper thing."

"Well . . ." She glanced at the clock.

"I promise I won't wander around the hallways," I said.

She folded her arms. "And?"

"And I won't go say hello to Mrs. Curtin and the kindergarteners even though saying hello to Mrs. Curtin is one of my most favorite things to do."

"Hmmm," she said. "And?"

"And I won't stop at every water fountain I see to get a drink." Then I added, "I only did that once."

She gave me a look. The I-don't-believe-you look.

"Okay," I said. "Maybe twice. But I was thirsty and I was in second grade." I stood up tall. "I'm much older now."

Finally, Mrs. Bingsley agreed. "Twenty minutes. Not a second longer."

I gave Mrs. Bingsley a hug and skedaddled down to the cafeteria. First stop: to visit the Penelope Parks painting.

"Sorry, Penelope. I'm through bidding on you. I need my money for something else. Someone else." I glanced at the last number on the list. #336: $17.00

"Who are you talking to, Katharine?" a voice asked.

"Mom! What are you doing here?"

"I work here, remember? What are you doing here?" She looked around the room. "Are you supposed to be here?"

"Don't worry. I'm on a top secret mission and it's approved by Mrs. Bingsley."

She smiled. "Well, then, don't let me stop you. Carry on!" Then she pointed to the Penelope Parks painting. "Does it have anything to do with that?"

"Sort of. But if I told you, it wouldn't be a top secret mission anymore. Besides, I'm not a blabbermouth. My lips are zipped."

"Good luck then," said Mom.

I waited until she went back into the kitchen before going over to the fifth grade tables. I found Crockett's box. There were only two bids:

#313: $1.00

#278: $3.00

I quickly wrote #100: $5.00. Then I erased my bid and wrote #100: $10.00 instead. Crockett was worth it. Way worth it. I walked around the room and looked for other items that I knew Crockett would like.

There were all sorts of things. Before I knew it, I had bid on a lizard tinfoil sculpture, a frame made out of twigs, and a clay magnet that said Reduce, Reuse, Recycle.

I wasn't even going to walk around the auction at lunch. But I decided to take one last looksie before recess. And I'm glad I did. Because I saw something terrible. Something that made me want to stomp and roar again.

Someone outbid me for Crockett's box. Didn't they know that today was Cheer Up Crockett Day?

Who bid on it?

#336. Gazillion Dollar Girl!

CHAPTER 7

Ammer the Hammer

After lunch, Mrs. Bingsley called us over to the carpet. "The auction is almost over. Final bids must be placed by three o'clock today," she announced.

I was hap, hap, happy to hear that! I was tired of the artsy-fartsy auction. I was also tired of being outbid by Miss Priss-A-Poo.

Maybe I had sour grapes, too.

"We've raised a lot of money so far," said Mrs. Bingsley. "Almost $800!"

I glared at Vanessa. Gazillion Dollar Girl probably bid $700.

"Our next auction is only four weeks away," said Mrs. Bingsley. "Five more of you will have the chance to donate your artwork. Hopefully, we'll raise even more money next time."

When I looked at Vanessa, she mouthed, "I'll raise more money than you."

That reminded me of my bowl! I had almost forgotten about it. My stomach did a flip-flop belly drop. I crossed my fingers. *Did anyone else bid on it?*

Mrs. Bingsley was still talking. Now she asked the class, "What charity would each of you like the money to go to?"

While everyone told Mrs. Bingsley who they thought our money should be donated to, I scooted over to Crockett.

"Do you want to go to Wing Li's for dinner tonight?" I asked. Then I added, "My treat."

"Do you have money left over from bidding?" asked Crockett. "Wing Li's is kind of expensive."

"Oops," I said. "Guess not. How about I treat next time?" Then I thought about how much Crockett loves ice cream. "Maybe we can go get some ice cream tonight instead? I'll ask my parents to take us."

Crockett squinted his eyes at me. "Katharine, if you're being extra nice to me because of my dad . . ."

I waved my hand through the air like I was waving away that idea. "That's not it. It's just that . . . well . . ." I stuttered.

Crockett leaned over and whispered, "Liar, liar pants on fire!"

I laughed. "Okay, okay. I do feel bad that your dad isn't coming this weekend. I know you miss him a lot. So I wanted to cheer you up a bit."

Crockett ran his fingers through his hair. "I'm kind of used to it. And I thought about what you said. Your dad is sort of like my dad."

"And your mom is like another mom to me," I said.

"Really?" asked Crockett. "That's kind of cool."

I gave Crockett a big old hug-a-rooni. "Then that makes me sort of like your sister. Not just your cousin. How cool is that?"

His face turned red as he scooted a few inches away from me. "You know how you don't like it when your mom hugs and kisses you in school and calls you Sweetie Pie?"

I nodded. "That drives me bonkers!"

He backed up another inch. And then another.

I folded my arms over my chest. “Am I driving you bonkers?” I asked. Then I whispered, “Sorry, Crockett. No more hugs. Promise.”

But I wasn’t sorry about my plan. It was working. Crockett smiled all day long.

Until writing workshop time. That’s when he got gloomy and glum again.

“Write about something you’re planning on doing over the weekend,” said Mrs. Bingsley.

“Can it be a made-up story?” asked Crockett.

“It should be something you’re going to do,” said Mrs. Bingsley. “If you don’t have plans yet, write about what you hope to do.”

Crockett frowned. He chewed on his pencil.

"Write about swim lessons," I said.

He made a face.

"How about your hike with Johnny and his dad?"

Crockett wrote his name on the paper. "Maybe."

But he didn't write anything else. Ten minutes later, he still had a blank piece of paper in front of him.

"Write about Movie Night," I said. Friday night was always movie night at our house.

He put his head down on his desk and closed his eyes. Finally, he asked to go to the nurse.

"I have a headache, Mrs. Bingsley," Crockett said quietly. "Can I go to the nurse?"

When I peeked at his paper a few minutes later, he only had a title: Making a Box with My Dad.

I glanced at the clock. It was 2:50. Time was ticking away. I knew I just had to be the last one to bid on that box!

Finally, at 2:55, I asked if I could go to the bathroom. "I'll be quicky quick. Promise."

"Now?" asked Mrs. Bingsley. "Can't you wait five minutes?"

"Nope. I can't." I jumped up and down. "I really need to go. *Now.*"

"Hurry up," said Mrs. Bingsley. "The bell's about to ring."

Since I didn't want to be a Cheatie Girl, I walked into the bathroom and washed my hands. Then, I rushed down to the cafeteria.

Before I went in, I looked around to make sure it was empty. I walked over to Crockett's box and wrote #100: $12.00. Ten seconds later, the bell rang. I won! That meant Crockett won!

I felt so super-duper, I wanted to burst.

I felt so super-duper that I drew a little happy face next to #336. Then I wrote, *Boo to You, Miss P-A-P. You are a C.G.*

Then I felt a tap, tap, tap on my shoulder. I turned around expecting to see Mom. But it wasn't my mom.

It was Mrs. Ammer.

Rats.

Ammer the Hammer nailed me again.

CROCKETT
KATHARINE

CHAPTER 8

One Smart Cookie

Mrs. Ammer led me into her office. "Haven't you been in here before for ruining school property?"

I nodded. "I de-eyed the *In the Spotlight* bulletin board when my mom started working here."

Mrs. Ammer looked confused. "De-eyed?"

I nibbled on my nail. "Maybe I de-nosed the bulletin board?" Then I sighed. "I think I de-mouthed the bulletin board."

Mrs. Ammer scratched her head. Then she slowly nodded. "You mean *defaced,* don't you?"

"That's it!" I shouted. "How could I forget that word?"

"You obviously did," said Mrs. Ammer. "You wrote a not-so-nice message on a bid paper."

My stomach did a flip-flop belly drop. "It was just an itty-bitty piece of paper. I didn't think it was school property. Honest." Then I started to cry.

I buried my face in my hands and put my head down on the desk. "I was just so mad this week. Mad at Vanessa. Mad at everyone who didn't bid on my artwork, and mad at Uncle Greg."

Mrs. Ammer handed me a tissue.

"Now I'm mad at myself that I'm back here visiting you again." I looked at the door. "And if my mom knew I was in here being so mad, she'd be mad at me."

"Take a deep breath, Katharine," said Mrs. Ammer. "Calm down."

But I couldn't calm down. I cried so much, she gave me the whole box of tissues!

Mrs. Ammer walked to her fridge in the corner and grabbed a water bottle. She handed it to me and asked, "Why are you mad about your bowl? Your bowl raised twenty-five dollars. That's a lot of money, isn't it?"

I stopped crying. I stopped sniffling. "Twenty-five dollars?" I whispered. "Are you sure?"

"Sure as can be," said Mrs. Ammer with a big goof-a-roo grin.

I didn't believe her. "Are you positively positive? Cross your heart?"

Mrs. Ammer laughed. "Positively positive, cross my heart."

Now it was her turn to whisper. "Want to know how certain I am that it sold for twenty-five dollars?"

"You betcha!" I said as I folded my legs under me.

"Because I bid on it, Katharine. I've decided I'm donating twenty-five dollars to each auction. After all, it's for a great cause. So I looked around the room and saw your popcorn bowl. My grandchildren will love it! I love it!"

I suddenly felt shiny and sparkly. Glittery and shimmery. I heart Mrs. Ammer!

"Is everything alright between you and your Uncle Greg? If not, you can talk to me. I'm a great listener," Mrs. Ammer said.

"I'm mad at Uncle Greg because Crockett is mad at him. At least I think he is." Then I explained. "Crockett is sad that he doesn't get to see his dad much. He wanted to make a box for Junior Rangers with him this weekend. All the other kids have a box for their compasses. But his dad called and had to cancel. Again."

"Oh, I see," said Mrs. Ammer. "But what does that have to do with the auction?"

"Everything," I said. "Crockett saw a perfect box for Junior Rangers. A fifth grader made it. It even said Junior Rangers on the lid. But when I went to bid on it, Vanessa outbid me. So, that's why I'm mad at her. Crockett needed that box."

Mrs. Ammer took a deep breath. "So you're mad at Vanessa because she outbid you on the box?"

I slowly nodded my head. Then I told her all about the Penelope Parks painting and #336.

"She told me she wasn't bidding on anything but she did. She's a Cheatie Girl."

Mrs. Ammer opened a folder on her desk. It was full of numbers and names. "I have the bid numbers here." She ran her finger down a list and smiled. "I'll be right back. Sit tight, Katharine."

A minute later, she returned with Crockett. He had two bags in his hands.

Mrs. Ammer took the bag marked Katharine out of his hand. She handed it to me. I opened it up and saw the box I had won! I also won the lizard sculpture and the magnet.

I shoved the bag back into his hands. "Crockett, this is for you. From me."

He peeked into the bag. "Are you serious?" He pulled out the box and jumped up and down. "I love it!"

"My dad wants to help you carve your name in it," I said. "This weekend."

Crockett couldn't stop smiling.

"There's more," I said. I showed him the magnet and the lizard sculpture. "I just don't get it, Crockett. Why didn't you bid on the box?"

"I did bid on it once yesterday. But I was too busy to go back and bid again because I was trying to win this." He held up a large bag. "It's for you."

"Me?" I said. "You bought me something? Why?"

He shrugged. "For lots of reasons. You organized the Red, White, and Blue Crew for me, didn't you? I wouldn't have won the election without you. And," he added, "because I knew you'd go bonkers over it."

He handed the bag to me.

"Can I open it?" I didn't wait for his answer. I ripped open the bag and gasped. It was the Penelope Parks painting!

"It's per-fect-o, Crockett. Fab-u-lo-so!" I jumped up and down. But only for a few seconds. "Wait a minute. I thought Vanessa won this."

"I told you before," said Crockett, "she said she wasn't bidding on anything. I kind of figured I was bidding against you for the painting. Are you number 100?"

I nodded. "But what number are you?" Then it hit me. Crockett was number 336! "I thought Vanessa was 336. I saw the slip of paper under her desk."

Crockett slapped his forehead. "That's where it went! It must have slipped out of my pocket. I looked all over for it!"

Then I thought about Vanessa. "I need to apologize to Vanessa. I wasn't very nice to her." Then I turned to Mrs. Ammer. "Am I in trouble?"

This is what I thought she'd say:

"Let's go get your mother so we can discuss a punishment."

But this is what she really said:

"I think we can keep this matter private because you've learned such an important lesson, haven't you?"

"I sure have," I said.

"About Vanessa?" asked Crockett.

I nodded. "But I also learned that it feels really, really good to buy something for someone else instead of yourself."

Mrs. Ammer agreed. "You know what, Katharine? I think you're one smart cookie."

And I felt like one, too.

A Per-fect-o Popcorn Bowl

Make a popcorn bowl just like Katharine's! You need: a balloon, newspaper, napkins, cardboard, a marker, scissors, water, glue, paint, paintbrushes, and two bowls.

1. Blow up a large balloon. Hold the tied end and use a marker to draw a line around your balloon to show how tall your bowl will be.
2. Cut a flat, round piece of cardboard. Glue it to the bottom of your balloon to make your bowl sturdy.
3. Flip the balloon so the tied part goes into a bowl. This makes it easy breezy to work on.
4. Mix equal parts glue and water in a bowl. Stir.
5. Cut strips of newspaper (1 inch by 6 inches) and dip them into the glue mixture. Place the strips to cover cardboard first and then the entire bottom half of balloon. Don't go above the marker line.
6. Let the layer dry, then glue on two more layers of paper and glue. Let them dry between layers.
7. Once completely dry, pop the balloon and peel it out of the bottom of the bowl.
8. Paint your bowl. Place a napkin inside and pour your favorite popcorn into it.